Potluck of the Draw

A Newfound Lake Cozy Mystery
Book 4

Virginia K. Bennett

To the members of the writing community who supported me early on, thank you!

Skye Jones
Marissa Farrar
Dawn Edwards
Kat Reads Romance
Kathryn LeBlanc
TL Swan
VR Tennent
Gina Sturino
Rachelle Kampen
...and so many more!

Table of Contents

Also by Virginia K. Bennett

A Newfound Lake Cozy Mystery:

Catch of the Day

A View From The Ledge

Once Inn A Lifetime

* * *

The Mysteries of Cozy Cove:

Much Ado About Muffin

It's All or Muffin

Muffin to Lose

Nothing Ventured, Muffin Gained

You Ain't Seen Muffin Yet

Here Goes Muffin

Chapter 1

The Potluck

"I think we're all ready to close up," Rebecca announced to Mary, the most reliable and eldest volunteer ever to work at the library.

"Dear, do you think I should stay while you head to the pasta dinner, just in case anyone missed the notices?" Mary was more committed to the readers of the Newfound community than anyone else Rebecca knew.

"If they missed the announcement on the doors and the counter and the social media posts for the last two weeks, it's on them. Thank you so much for your efforts and enjoy the weekend. Do you have any plans?"

"None at all, except to stay home from tonight until Sunday morning when I head to church. I want nothing to do with all the extra traffic and festivities." She picked up two new cozy mysteries Rebecca just entered into the system today. "I'll have these back when I get here on Monday, promise."

"If not, we'll just have to revoke your library card," Rebecca replied sternly.

"Well, then you'll need to find yourself another free employee." Mary winked and walked toward the front door. "Good luck transporting that sauce." She waved an arm above her head before leaving.

Rebecca had four crockpots of pasta sauce ready to go to the pre-marathon potluck dinner in Kelley Park. Having retrieved two crockpots from her basement, she added them to the two she borrowed from Mary and Karen. Earlier, she filled them with all the necessary ingredients so they would be ready to bring with her to donate to the Mason's pasta supper. Previously, the supper was held indoors, but there was no longer enough room for everyone who wanted to participate. The Masons were using the kitchen inside the community center for cooking the pasta this year.

The crockpots at home had been cooking on low since this morning and would be ready to serve right on time for the dinner. She was happy to support both the runners and the Masons by cooking. Since she was not about to lace up her trainers and run the marathon herself, this was the next best thing. Tomorrow, she would be manning one of the tables at a water station in front of Shanty's, which was now closed until next summer.

Fall was descending upon the sleepy towns that surround Newfound Lake. Many local spots had already closed, like Catch of the Day, while others were usually hitting their stride. Apple orchards were hit hard by a late frost in May, so there were nowhere near as many farms available for picking. They did, however, have many other things to offer locals and leaf peepers. The marathon runners were part of the extended tourist season that kept the towns running through the end of September.

Rebecca took one last look around the library which would be closed from three on Friday afternoon through Monday morning. She would be volunteering at the marathon, but also wanted to free up parking spaces that would be so desperately needed. With over five hundred runners competing, the surrounding towns would be bulging at the seams. Restaurants like Jilly's would be hustling every moment they were open, catering to the regular customers and visitors who only saw the marathon as a way to qualify for the Boston Marathon.

Driving home, she realized she would need to come up with one more box to transport the final crockpot of sauce. Her basement was a plethora of random items she just might need some day, so she felt confident there would be something down there that fit the size requirements.

Directly behind the front door sat her two black cats, Joey and Bean, ready for some attention. "How did you two know I would be home early?" she asked, knowing there would be no verbal response. "Do you think a few treats would be in order?" The cats circled her feet as she attempted to make her way to the treats without stepping on them. With bellies full of seafood-flavored yumminess and food dishes topped off, Rebecca accepted they no longer required her attention and moved to the sink with their water dishes. Once filled, she proceeded to the basement to acquire the final box for the sauce crockpots.

She made sure not to add up the cost of the donation because it was sure to be more than she realized, given that she picked up ingredients little by little over several shopping trips. She reached the top of the basement stairs and closed the door behind her. On the rare occasion her little bundles of fur managed to make it down there, they inevitably returned with a wiggling treat as a present for her – a present she did not want. She unplugged the crockpots, assigned them each to a box and carried them out to the back of her green Subaru. This was one of many times she was glad she had a practical hatchback. Returning to the house long enough to change out of her shirt a frequent patron made for her – In My Librarian Era – and into last year's volunteer shirt, she quickly headed back to her car and drove to Kelley Park.

When she got to North Main Street, she realized she was going to have a difficult time finding anywhere to park closer than the library itself. She pulled into the bank parking lot in the center of town and called Kenny, her new significant other and Chief of Police.

"Hello, beautiful. I thought you'd be at the pasta supper by now."

"I'm headed there but can't find anywhere to park other than the back parking lot of the bank. Is that okay since they're closed?"

He chuckled over the phone. "I promise to cancel the ticket if you get one. Need any help unloading?"

"I'd love some. Where are you?" She heard a knock on the passenger window. In full uniform, Kenny was smiling from ear to ear.

"Right here." He disconnected the call and opened the door. "How can I help?"

"There are four crockpots and some ladles that need to get to the pavilion."

He walked around to the back of the car and popped open the hatchback. The car was too old to have a button for Rebecca to open it for him, so she joined him as soon as she turned the key to shut the car off. "We'll need to make two trips, but that's certainly better than four. Thank you." She stood up on her toes to kiss him on the cheek as he held the first box.

"Not a problem, young lady. Always happy to help the volunteers that support the marathon." After grabbing her own box and shutting the back, they walked beside each other across the street and down the road to Kelley park.

Large white tents stood in the outfield of the baseball diamond with tables and chairs ready for hungry racers and their guests. Rebecca had a moment where she imagined the old grandstand still in place across the field. She knew it was removed because it was dangerous, but it was such a fond childhood memory. The carnival would come to town behind that grandstand, and kids would play on it late into the night. She was sure more than one visit to the hospital was due to the lack of supervision in that structure.

After returning with the remaining boxes and utensils, Kenny headed out, walking in the direction of his cruiser in the parking lot behind the bank. Rebecca began unboxing and plugging in the crockpots of sauce at her assigned table space.

The woman in charge of the assignments was Marilyn. Her husband was a Mason, but everyone knew this was Marilyn's show to run. Rebecca had reserved four outlets last week according to Marilyn's schedule. While people may have made fun of her organization behind her back, everyone knew the event would run without a hitch due to her detailed approach.

"Marilyn, I found my table space and four outlets. Thank you for your efforts."

"Thank you for showing up on time and prepared. That certainly does make my job easier." She held up a clipboard and checked something off. "Joel, what are you doing a table six? I have you scheduled to be at table two. Sorry, Rebecca, duty calls."

"No problem. Good luck." Marilyn hustled over to Joel with his two crockpots at table six to make sure to remedy the situation promptly, her hips swaying as she power walked.

As predicted, the rest of the evening went smoothly. There was a printed menu of choices Marilyn had assembled at the start of the tables so runners knew which crockpots to look for. Rebecca's sauce had no sugar and no meat and was blended so there would be no chunks. She figured if that's the way Kenny liked it, there must be other no-chunk people in the world. As sauces ran out,

Marilyn adjusted the menu so no one would be surprised.

The clean-up process went quickly due to Marilyn's recruitment of a crew to do just that. Within thirty minutes of the last people finishing, everything was ready to be picked up by the rental company, though the tents were scheduled to stay up all weekend.

"Thanks for all your hard work tonight," shouted Marilyn as people began to head out. "Don't forget to get here bright and early tomorrow to get your shirts and location assignments. Traffic will be a nightmare if you are late."

* * *

Bright and early the next morning, Rebecca picked up her volunteer shirt and received her assignment. This year, she would be manning the water table in front of Shanty's. They were closed for the season, but provided a nice space for runners to get what they needed late in the race. She knew she would be seeing runners from the half-marathon first, but looked forward to the three locals who were predicted to take the top spots again this year.

While there were many runners who came to Newfound Lake for the New Hampshire Marathon just to qualify for Boston, locals also ran for the bragging rights.

The runner she was looking forward to seeing most was Jeremy. He wasn't expected to win anything other than his age group, 65 and up, but Rebecca looked forward to cheering on one of her library volunteers. Elise Trussell and Jenny Lipman were the two big names in the women's race this year. Elise won last year, and Jenny came in third. The woman who came in second happened to be volunteering at the Shanty's water table with Rebecca. Kennedy Wright placed second last year but ended up needing to have knee surgery early in the spring and couldn't be competitive in the marathon so soon.

Rebecca pulled into the parking lot of Shanty's on the lake side of West Shore Road and parked her Subaru. She grabbed a bag with sunscreen, extra layers and a change of socks and shoes. She favored flip flops, but the day would be long, possibly too long to completely forgo sneakers. In addition, she packed some of her favorite snacks in a small lunch bag.

"Kennedy, nice to see you here. Just couldn't stay away?" She noticed the second-place finisher from last year ambling in her direction as she finished placing the last of the supplies that would fit on the table.

"It is killing me to not run the marathon, but I know I'm not ready. My physical therapist said I could if I wanted to, but I'd need to take it easy."

"The Kennedy I know wouldn't be able to take it easy," Rebecca jested.

"That's why I'm not running. Are we all set, or can I help with anything?" Kennedy looked around, her long, wavy ponytail swishing from side to side.

If anyone should have been competing in the marathon today, it was Kennedy. She'd been in the local newspaper countless times throughout high school for every sport you could think of. The Newfound Regional High School gymnasium was filled with banners including her name. Coming in second last year had been a shock, but the winner was no slouch.

Elise Trussell had moved to the Newfound area after getting her Bachelor of Science degree in Park and Recreation Management. She took a job with the New Hampshire Division of Parks and Recreation working at Wellington state park straight out of college. If she wasn't working outdoors, she was running or cross-country skiing.

Coming in third last year was Jenny Lipman, a woman about Rebecca's age who consistently placed in the top ten for women of any age. Now that she was over forty, she dominated her category. Her third-place finish had been the highest she'd ever achieved. Having visited Rebecca in the library before, she'd talked about how this was going to be her year. She had trained harder and wanted it more than ever.

"If you wanted to get those ropes up to keep others from pulling into the parking lot, that would be helpful. I'm going to start grabbing extras of everything for under the table. It won't be long before we'll have runners coming through here, just not from the marathon."

Kennedy slouched her shoulders as she walked over to the ropes Rebecca had mentioned, the lack of pep evident in every movement. "I'm on it."

Once several more volunteers showed up to help and the tables for snacks were all set up, the racers started showing up and time flew. Some bodies whizzed by, not interested in stopping for a drink, while others slowed down, or were already pretty slow, and sipped while running in place or stretching.

"Here she comes," yelled a volunteer farther up the road. "It's Jenny!"

Everyone shouted and hollered for the local celebrity as she passed. It was then that Kennedy spoke.

"But where is Elise?"

Chapter 2

The Search

"I'm sure we just missed her, or maybe she's injured," supplied Kennedy.

"Well, the official leader car is in front of Jenny, so we know we didn't miss her, but I guess she could be injured or have fallen behind." Rebecca continued to crane her neck to look for Elise. Something just wasn't sitting right with her. "If she's fallen much further behind, she won't stand a chance of catching Jenny."

"You don't want Jenny to win?" Kennedy inquired.

"Absolutely not what I'm implying. I want the best runner to win, so it just seems like Jenny and Elise should be closer than this." With every second that passed, Rebecca became more concerned about Elise. "I'm going to call Kenny."

Rebecca took her cell phone out of her back pocket to dial Kenny, and Kennedy pulled hers out as well, but the service was low. Rebecca's call wouldn't go through, so she sent a text.

Rebecca: We haven't seen Elise, but Jenny passed by maybe two minutes ago.

Rebecca: Any news on where Elise is in the pack?

Three dots popped up then disappeared. They popped up again and stayed longer, but they disappeared again. She continued searching the runners for Elise while still offering water to the current runners. Another minute went by before the phone in her hand vibrated.

Kenny: I've heard from the previous water station, and they saw her

Kenny: She was about thirty seconds behind Jenny at that time

Kenny: Are you sure you didn't just miss her?

Rebecca: Very sure. We were checking everywhere as soon as we saw Jenny.

Kenny: I'll let you know when I hear anything XOXO

Though the situation was tense, she smiled at the sign off. Kenny and Rebecca had become closer over the past month. They had gone on a few local dates, and she had even spent some time in Kelley park with Kenny when the girls were with him. There had been no discussion of her being dad's new girlfriend, but it didn't seem like that was far off. He had been a complete gentleman on every occasion. His ex-wife, Heather, knew about them and had explicitly told Kenny that she was happy he was dating someone she knew enough about to feel comfortable around the girls. On one more occasion before school started, the four of them had attended Rebecca's reading group together.

"Rebecca, still no Elise," reported Kennedy. "Now I'm really starting to get nervous."

The two women continued to look for the next five minutes before Rebecca finally crossed the road to see if anyone on the other side, in front of The Shanty Shack, had any news. She asked up and down the row of gawkers, but no one had seen her.

When she returned to the water table, Kennedy asked, "Well, any luck?"

"None. Nobody has seen her, and most hadn't noticed she was missing from the race. I'm going to text Kenny again." As soon as she retrieved her phone, his message popped up.

Kenny: No one working or volunteering can confirm her location since the last water station

Kenny: We're going to start asking runners that have finished what they know

Kenny: Keep watching for her

Rebecca decided she was going to do more than just stand here and wait. "Kennedy, what do you think about me walking the course backward to find Elise?"

"What do you mean?"

"We both seem pretty confident she hasn't passed by us, right?"

Kennedy squinted her eyes at Rebecca and tilted her head. "Right."

"Kenny, Chief Towne, reported that she did check in at a previous water station. If something happened, I should come across her between those two points." Rebecca looked at Kennedy with her arms open and palms up. "It stands to reason that other runners would probably check in with her, and she'd say she was fine so they would continue on. Maybe she doesn't want to ask for help because that would impact the times for the other racers."

"Seems logical. At this point, we mainly have only marathon runners going by. Other racers would be past us by now. Want me to go with you?"

"Let's check in with the other volunteers around this station to see if they can redistribute who is at which table."

Rebecca walked up to volunteers at the snack station where they were slowly handing out bars and things to unhurried runners. She was able to round up a couple people willing to shift to the water table so she and Kennedy could walk in the direction Elise should have come from.

Once everyone was in place, and after Rebecca changed into her socks and sneakers, the pair of women headed in the direction of the old Frosty's Corner. There was nothing worth noting on this stretch. They cheered on runners who looked at them quizzically, some briefly referencing who Kenndey was to the racing community as they went by. They traveled on the side of the road that would eventually be nearest the lake once they turned right. The other side of the road was mostly visible or above the level of the pavement, and this side was marked for the runners.

"Kennedy, is there any other scenario for Elise's absence?" Rebecca asked after walking in silence for a while. She took a swig of water, wishing she had thought to bring a bigger bottle.

"Well, what if she was picked up by someone driving. There would be no one to report to if she was injured and needed to get to a hospital. I mean, I know what it's like to blow out my knee. The last thing I would be thinking of was notifying anyone that I was out of the race. That pain was indescribable." Kennedy grimaced as she continued along the road.

After another long walk in silence, and well past the entrance to Wellington State Park at this point, they could see the lake again on their right. They continued to be passed by runners, but they were fewer and farther between now. Rebecca mostly enjoyed the view of the open water.

Next, they passed some small camps and a variety of fencing, and then there was a small area with a patch of trees between the road and the lake. Rebecca spotted the soles of a pair of running shoes amongst the green, but only because she was looking over the edge. Anyone focused on running the marathon would pass by without noticing a thing.

"Kennedy. Look!" She pointed to the pair of sneakers which were up off the ground, balanced on thick bushes. They jumped off the pavement and into the shrubbery. "Oh no!"

Rebecca could quickly see the shoes were attached to the legs of a person who was upside down, head against the base of a large tree, neck bent at an odd angle.

15

"Is it Elise?" Kennedy asked, still sounding hopeful that it wasn't.

Rebecca felt for a pulse first. "Either way, it's not looking good," she responded.

Together, they brought down the legs of the runner and gasped in unison. The badly damaged head of Elise Trussell came into view.

"Kennedy, you check for a pulse too, just in case I was wrong."

She did as she was asked and dropped her head, ponytail falling over her shoulder. Her shoulders shook. "She's gone."

The two women sat on the ground for a moment next to the body of someone who was going to be missed by both the local community and the greater running community.

"She should have been up there with Jenny on the podium. The race might even be over by now."

Rebecca took out her phone, intending to check the time, but checked for service instead. Not in any better condition than at Shanty's, she sent off a text to Kenny.

Rebecca: We found Elise. She's dead.

Rebecca: Bring an ambulance and your team.

Rebecca: We're in the trees past the Wellington Entrance and past the 30mph sign

Rebecca: Keep going past the brown camps and fencing. We'll be on the side of the road.

Rebecca watched a little symbol under the series of text messages pop up to notify her they hadn't gone through yet.

"One of us should walk back toward Frosty's Corner to make sure the message goes through," Rebecca suggested.

"That will take too long. Let's flag down a car and ask them to call as soon as they can."

They trudged back to the pavement, and, after a few cars, one finally stopped. They passed along the message and Kenny's phone number to the driver, asking them to stop at the Shanty's water station if their phone call hadn't gone through yet. There were people there who could get through to emergency personnel even if cell service wasn't working. Either way, they needed to get the message out to someone as quickly as possible.

"What do we do now?" Kennedy asked.

"I'm not sure. We don't know how she got down there, and it would seem that no one else saw it happen since the police didn't know when we were still at the volunteer station. We must be the first on the scene."

"I'm going to stay on the road, if you don't mind. I just can't keep looking at her like that." Kennedy looked like she might throw up.

"One of us needs to be there so the emergency team can find us. I'm going to stay with Elise."

What Rebecca didn't say was that she wanted to look at the scene, see if she could pick up on anything before everyone came tromping through here. She noticed the distance from the road to the final landing place. Rebecca's assessment was that there was no way she fell this far on her own and hit her head hard enough to cause this amount of damage. An accident like tripping or pulling a muscle seemed like it was not a plausible explanation.

As she walked around to the other side of Elise's body, she noticed a lot of damage to her side. Having run the marathon in only a sports bra due to the unseasonably warm temperatures this morning, about one foot of her torso was clearly visible. There was already some bruising and other lacerations. Based on the way they found her body, that damage didn't appear to have been caused by the tree.

Rebecca scurried back to where Kennedy sat. "Did you notice her side?"

Kennedy was sitting with her arms across her bent knees and her forehead balanced atop them. She rolled her head left then right. "No. What about her side?"

"Don't worry about it. If you didn't notice anything, that's fine. Want me to sit with you?"

"Sure."

Not for the first time today, they were together in silence. Kennedy clearly wasn't about to engage in any search for clues, and Rebecca didn't really have much else to go on. While they sat, she watched a few slow runners pass by and some cars in either direction. Her eyes were drawn to the pavement they were sitting on. It appeared to Rebecca that there were tire tracks in the dust and pebbles on the road continuing off the road to the dirt adjacent to the shoulder but didn't touch the grass after that. She didn't bring it to Kennedy's attention, but wanted to make sure any emergency vehicles didn't disturb what could be evidence.

After a few more minutes, the two could hear sirens, and those were quickly followed by the emergency vehicles rounding the bend. Rebecca flagged them down and stood in the center of the road so she could explain what she had seen. EMTs got out of the ambulance and ran in the direction she pointed to, but police officers, including Chief Towne, followed her to where she thought she may have found tire tracks.

"That's a great catch. I'm glad you protected this," stated Chief Towne."

"I don't know if it's connected to Elise in any way, but I'd rather your team got a chance to look at it first."

"We really appreciate it." He smiled, gave her shoulder a squeeze and walked in the direction of the officer cordoning off the area.

Rebecca felt at a loss. She knew there was nothing else she could do here but had no car and no way to call for a ride. Kennedy was in the same position. She chased after Kenny and gently grasped his arm.

He swung around quickly, startling her. "What's the problem?" he inquired.

"Can you help Kennedy and I figure out how to get back to Shanty's?"

Chapter 3

The Repercussions

KENNY FOUND AN OFFICER TO TRANSPORT REBECCA and Kennedy back to Shanty's, but not until after they had both given their statements. Kennedy was questioned by a different officer, but Rebecca assumed she was asked similar questions.

"How did you come upon the body?" the officer, who looked like he graduated from Newfound Regional High School back in June, asked.

"Kennedy and I noticed that Elise hadn't run past us and wasn't the leader, which we both assumed she would be. When I contacted Chief Towne to see if he knew where she was or if she was injured, he responded that he had no information. Eventually, he reported that she had been seen at one of the previous water stations, but not since. Kennedy and I decided to walk the course backward and look for her since we felt no one else was."

With the end of the pen at his mouth, he asked, "What made you think to look for her here?"

"Really, we had been looking all along the course. There was nowhere for her to hide on the other side of the road, and it would have been the opposite side she was running on. While we were getting dirty looks from runners, we figured she'd be on this side if anything happened to her."

"Why did you assume something had happened to her?" he asked after a long pause.

"I just explained that. We only knew she had been seen at a previous water station, so it seemed logical she was either injured along the course or had been picked up and transported somewhere. If we found nothing, you could be calling Speare Memorial." Rebecca was getting frustrated, and she hoped her long, audible exhales where being heard by the officer. She had often been picked on for her red hair, being told she was a fiery redhead, and today she felt like one.

"Why this grouping of trees?"

At a volume that turned Kenny's head from several yards away, she stated, "We checked all of the trees, and beaches, and fences, and yards. We were looking for her with a purpose. Dozens of runners, at least, passed right by her and never noticed her because they weren't looking for her. They had no reason to look for her. Most of the runners assumed she'd be way ahead of them. We had a reason to look for her." She looked up and spotted Kenny staring at her. He took a long, slow deep breath and pushed his downturned hand from neck to waist high. Rebecca responded by taking a long, slow deep breath.

"Ma'am, I'm trying to gather as much information as possible. I know you understand that, and I'm not trying to frustrate you." He looked nervous and kept checking over his shoulder to look at Chief Towne. She wondered what he was checking for.

"I'm not angry at you. I'm upset that she's dead and I'm still here. It's not your fault." She too checked on Chief town. "Can I go now," she shouted to him.

Kenny sauntered over to the officer interviewing Rebecca. "Jacob, did you get everything you needed?"

"Yes, sir. Just finished up."

"Could you please drive Rebecca and Kennedy back to Shanty's. It looks like Kennedy is done as well." Kenny didn't give her a kiss or a look or a squeeze. He went back to work. Rebecca was grown up enough to know he wasn't dismissing her; he was being professional. She'd get to see him later.

Rebecca walked over to Kennedy and wrapped an arm around her. Before the water station, they hadn't been friends or even acquaintances. Rebecca knew who Kennedy was from the previous marathon and the story in the paper last week. Today, she was consoling her because they had been through something together.

"Let's go back," Kennedy suggested, quietly. They walked to the cruiser with the officer known as Josh, but his badge read Whitaker. Riding in the back seat, the only noise was Kennedy sniffling. When he pulled into Shanty's, there were still runners collecting water as they traveled toward their destination.

"Do you need a ride home?" Rebecca asked.

"No. I can have someone pick me up."

"Feel free to stop by the library on Monday if you want to talk. Want my phone number?"

Kennedy appeared to think about it. "I'm all set, but thanks." She ambled to the other side of the road. Several minutes passed before she took out her phone, but she never brought it to her ear. Rebecca assumed she sent a text instead of attempting a call with the unpredictable cell service. When a vehicle pulled into the space next to the Shanty Shack, she got up and got in. The driver attempted to pull out onto West Shore Road a few times, and it took a bit. She gave a pathetic wave to Rebecca as they left.

While Rebecca stayed for another hour, she didn't say one word to any of the other volunteers. No one around her knew what she had seen, and it wasn't her place to tell them. When they were ready to thin out the help, she put her hand up and asked to go home.

It felt better than she expected to lay on her living room floor and cuddle her four-legged babies. Joey and Bean rubbed her face and elbows and knees, waiting to get pet in return, but she didn't move until she started to cry. There was no previous connection or long-term adoration for Elise, but she was now gone. Kenny would be required to call her family and tell them she wasn't coming home. Rebecca couldn't come to terms with the fact she was responsible for that phone call. She was the cause of ultimate suffering today. With her two cats beside her, she cried on her floor until she fell asleep.

Knock, knock, knock. "Rebecca, are you in there?"

Rebecca began to stir, not knowing the day or time. Her back and neck hurt, but she didn't know why. She looked around and noticed it was dark, both inside and outside. She looked around again then lifted herself up onto her elbows. The cats, who had been sleeping against each side, woke with a start. They jumped again when another series of knocks rang through the living room. "Why am I here?" She stood up and her front door swung open at the same time.

"Where have you been, and why haven't you responded to my texts and calls?" Kenny placed a box on the small table just inside the front door and wrapped his arms around her, kissing her temple and forehead. "Are you alright?"

She stood in his embrace for a minute before pulling back so she could look up at him. She took in his concerned gaze, his hair turning gray and the wrinkles around the corners of his eyes. "Today just made me think about how quickly life can be taken away. I don't know why the other deaths didn't affect me like this, but this one hit hard. I don't even know how long I slept on the floor. Oh no! Joey and Bean must be so hungry." She quickly moved to the kitchen where her two black cats waited patiently near their food bowls. After feeding them and giving them some extra love, she realized Kenny had been watching her from a kitchen stool in full uniform.

"I brought some food." He held up the box. "Didn't know if you needed dinner when you weren't answering. If not, I can leave."

There was no way she wanted him to leave. "What's in the box?"

"I know it's not your favorite, but Jilly's wasn't open this late." He opened the box to reveal two calzones and some fried pickle spears. "The only condition is that you don't make me watch Sweet Home Alabama again." He held the box away from her reach as she extended her arms, waiting for an agreement.

"Deal." He handed the box over, and she said, "I was thinking Maid in Manhattan anyway." She winked and carried the box over to the oven. After turning the oven on, she removed a baking sheet from the drawer under the oven and transferred the calzones and pickles to it. Even though it was still pre-heating, she placed the food into the oven.

"While I'm not usually opposed to chick flicks, I can't stay that long."

"Do you have the girls tonight?" she asked, looking down at the surface of the counter, hands holding her head up.

"No. They are with Heather. I have a mountain of work ahead of me. We have virtually no evidence to go by. Your descriptions, however, were very helpful. Unofficially, we are confident she was hit by a car and that's how she ended up off the road and against that tree." Rebecca could feel his eyes boring into the top of her head, so she looked up.

"How do you solve a..." She paused. "Was it a murder?"

"We have every reason to believe it was a homicide,

though we don't know if it was a hit and run or purposeful. I'm not sure which I'm hoping for."

"She was in her prime. I'm not just talking about running. She was young. She had her whole life ahead of her. She hadn't had the job at Wellington long. All of that, gone in an instant. At least, I hope it was over quickly. Did anyone say if they thought she suffered?"

"We don't know anything like that yet."

The oven beeped, letting them know it had reached the desired temperature. Before checking it, Rebecca gathered plates, utensils, glasses and the ranch dressing. "What do you want to drink?"

"I'm good with just water, thanks."

Rebecca was starting to feel a little more like herself. The part of her brain that needed this death to be part of a complete story finally began to whirl. She poured the water and asked, "Did the marks I found mean anything? Were they helpful?"

"That's another thing we don't know. We took measurements and pictures, and they would absolutely be evidence in a court case. Now we need to see if we can piece together a motive or means if this was on purpose."

"If it wasn't, and there is no other evidence, someone is going to get away with murder, even if they didn't mean to."

Kenny shook his head and frowned. "That does happen. Sometimes there just isn't anything we can do. If there are no cameras, no witnesses and no evidence, a crime like this can go unsolved. Chances are, that's why it happened where it did."

"What do you mean? Wait, let me get food first." She grabbed two potholders and removed the baking sheet from the oven, turning it off. She transferred each calzone to a plate. "How do I know which one is mine?" I ordered one with mushrooms and one with ham and pineapple, so it doesn't matter. We can cut them in half and share if you want."

She smiled. His thoughtfulness always surprised her, though it shouldn't. He was a thoughtful man who had a long night ahead of him, and he still came to check in on her and bring her dinner.

"Why did you say that about where it happened?"

"Just that there aren't any cameras pointing there. Maybe it was an accident or maybe they just got lucky, but not one place in that area had a camera facing the road anywhere near where you found Elise."

"Figures," she summed up.

They enjoyed their dinner while she recapped the earlier part of the day. He also told her about his traffic detail in town which was much less exciting.

"I know I just got here, but I need to get going. I have a lot of footage to watch, and not enough officers to assign it to."

Rebecca snapped to attention. "But you just said there were no cameras in the area. What footage are you going to watch?"

"Shanty's has security cameras, so we can try that to see if a car goes by with front-end damage. The other officers are still out checking in both directions for any cameras that may have caught a car heading to the scene

27

without damage and leaving with damage. It's going to be a long and arduous process, but it's the only thing we can go on."

Rebecca wished she could get her eyes on that footage, but she knew that was a battle she wouldn't win.

"I don't want to keep you. Get going so you can go home at a reasonable time. Leave your stuff on the counter."

He did as she instructed. "I'll do my best." They headed to her front door where he turned around and wrapped her in his arms again.

"You seem much better than when I got here. Is that accurate?" he asked, still showing concern for her wellbeing.

"I'm better, and I'm going to clean up then go to sleep. I have to be rested for my day off tomorrow. She chuckled. "Good night."

He leaned in for a kiss. "Good night, sweetheart. See you tomorrow."

Chapter 4

The Ranger

Rebecca fell asleep quickly, but it was a restless sleep. She dreamt of searching for something she couldn't find, finding the body of Elise over and over again, and opening the door for Kenny when he wasn't there. She kept looking at the clock each time she woke up, and it seemed she was only sleeping – if you could call it that – about twenty minutes at a time. Exhausted and frustrated, she got up and started cleaning the house around four in the morning.

Today was her day off, though she hadn't been to the library since Friday afternoon. She could only imagine how full the drop box would be Monday, but that was the least of her concerns. How would she ever begin to help find Elise's killer with no evidence, motive or theories? Kenny hadn't been any help last night, other than confirming her observation regarding the damage to Elise's torso.

"If she was hit by a car, and it really was an accident, no amount of questioning will help unless someone decides to confess," Rebecca said aloud while Bean and Joey watched her clean the oven. "I'm sure, based on what Kenny said, they are focusing on camera footage for clues. I can't help with that, so maybe I should do what I think they will do last." She dropped her back side onto the floor after so much kneeling and scrubbing. "I'll see if I can get into Wellington and talk to the people she worked with."

Rebecca knew, like any local did, that Wellington was closed for the season. Kids were back in school, summer camps were over and tourists had mostly returned to their regular homes. While Newfound was in the middle of the most beautiful foliage week of the year, the beach didn't need to be open for that. During the height of summer, the beach filled up fast and parking was difficult to come by, but the challenge today would be different.

When she finished the oven, she went to her room and pulled out a pair of jean capris and paired them with a Red Sox t-shirt – a navy blue one so it didn't clash with her red hair – and returned to the first floor for her sneakers. She looked around the house, admiring how clean it was. If Kenny showed up unannounced, she would be ready.

Her trusty green Subaru made the familiar trip along West Shore Road. When she pulled into the driveway for Wellington, the wooden gates prevented her from getting into the parking lot. She left a note with her contact information on the dash in case someone thought it had been abandoned. Getting out of her car, she remembered to grab her water bottle.

The walk past the booth to pay reminded her of all the years she came here as a little girl, ready to swim until they kicked her out. Walking through a deserted parking lot, however, was unfamiliar and unnerving. She walked down a still path, devoid of shrieks of laughter from children on their way to play all day. When the path opened up, the bathhouses came into view, followed by the beautiful lake.

Off to her left came the sound of banging. If she was going to talk to someone, it made the most sense to head toward the noise. It didn't take long for Rebecca to find a man, probably in his late twenties, swinging a hammer. The picnic table looked like it had been around longer than he had, but he was making a valiant attempt to revive it. She had never thought about work the went on once the park closed for the summer.

"Excuse me," she shouted. He jumped when he looked up, probably because she was only about ten feet in front of him at that point.

"Hey, I'm pretty sure you're about two weeks late. We're just doing some maintenance at this point in the season."

"That's fine. I'm actually here to talk to you, if that's okay. Name's Rebecca." She walked the final steps to be able to reach across the table to offer her hand.

When he accepted the gesture, he replied, "I'm Franklin, but most people call me Frank."

"That name seems older than you are. Were you named after someone?"

"My father and grandfather, actually. I'm a third," he said, brushing imaginary dirt off his shoulder.

"Well, look at you." She smiled, hands in her pockets, rocking back and forth from toe to heel.

"What did you want to talk to me about? Have a seat," he offered, sitting down on the bench he was just repairing.

Rebecca looked into his eyes, reading him as an honest person from the start. She only hoped her gut was telling the truth. "Frank, did you know Elise Trussell?" He immediately frowned and looked down at the table in front of him.

"I did. Why do you ask?" His voice now a whisper compared to the jovial one she was introduced to.

She accepted the invitation to sit and straddled the bench seat. "I was the one who found her during the marathon. I was with Kennedy Wright, another local runner, and we noticed Elise hadn't passed by us. We were at the water station in front of Shanty's. Once Jenny passed with the lead car, we expected to see Elise but didn't." Though she wasn't done with her explanation, she stopped. "Frank, are you okay?"

Frank had begun to cry. "No, not really. I'm trying to put on a good face and keep busy, but I'm not doing well."

"Were you and Elise close?"

"I had a crush on her, but she was my co-worker. I wanted to wait until the off-season, then I wanted to wait until she finished the marathon, but now I can't tell her."

Rebecca placed a hand on top of his, hoping to soothe a little of his pain or maybe give him some of her strength.

"I wanted to wait to ask her out. I was hoping we might have a chance to date in the fall. I can't believe she's gone. I mean, less than twenty-four hours gone." He continued to cry and wipe his face but not openly sob.

"Oh, Frank, I'm so sorry. That must be such a hard group of emotions to process."

"In the last couple of weeks, we spent so much time talking about how she was training for the marathon and her plan during the race so she could repeat her win and hopefully beat her personal record. There are just so many unresolved...things." He was struggling to hold sentences together. It was evident now she was looking at his eyes up close that he was younger than Rebecca first assessed.

"This is surely going to take a lot of time to process if you felt that way about her and never got to tell her."

"I know, but I *will* get to process those feelings. She never got to finish the race. She never got to get married or have kids or grow old with someone. Somebody took that away from her."

"Do you have any idea what happened to her?"

"She was telling me she felt like she was being followed, and I told her it was just nerves because of the race coming up. Now, that's another thing that I will have to live with." Frank put his head down on his arms and continued to cry.

"Did she say why she thought she was being followed?"

He lifted his head and tried to breathe through the tears to speak again. "She thought she was being followed twice when driving home, and a couple times here she thought someone was watching her."

"Did she report it to anyone or tell you about the car following her?"

"You sure are asking a lot of questions." His sad, grieving demeanor gave way to a look of suspicion. "Who are you to Elise, other than being the one who found her?"

"Just a concerned citizen. I'm worried the police are up to their elbows in other parts of her case, and I don't want anything to get missed. If I hadn't come here to ask, they might never have known she felt like she was being followed, for instance." She crossed her arms and gave a slightly proud huff. "And, yes, I did find her. That is something I can never unsee. I want whoever ended her life to be held accountable appropriately."

"I'm sorry. I didn't think about how you were feeling." Frank sniffled and wiped the back of his hand under his nose.

"No apology needed. We're going through very different feelings, and I know asking questions makes me feel less helpless. It's probably the same reason you're working on picnic tables today."

"Probably. What did you ask me last?"

Rebecca thought for a moment. "Right, did she tell you anything about the car following her?"

"I never said car. It was a truck or SUV, she thought, but that must have been all she could make out because she only saw it in her rearview mirror."

"If she only saw it in her mirror, it mustn't have followed her home." Rebecca was trying to replicate a scene based on the memory of a memory, and an emotional one at that.

"She said it stopped before she got to her house. Does that help?" The glimmer in his eyes seemed to flash for just a moment.

"It could. I think it would really help if you told everything you told me to Chief Towne. He's heading up the investigation, and what you know just might be enough to help with camera footage, if you can narrow a few things down. Would you be willing to do that?"

"Sure. I'd do anything for Elise."

"Well, footage from residential cameras gets deleted pretty quickly, so the faster you can get what you know to the police, the better their chances are of getting eyes on it." Rebecca wasn't sure just how long camera recordings lasted, but she knew her doorbell camera was only a few hours. Since she didn't know where Elise lived, they might be running out of time for even business cameras to still have video from someone following her.

"I'll go now. Want to walk out with me? I mean, I shouldn't leave you here."

Rebecca laughed. "I think it's best if I head out too. I got lucky you were here. Hopefully our luck will continue."

They stood at the same time and headed toward the

dark green pickup truck Frank must have been using as a park ranger. He grabbed his hammer and walked to the passenger side of the truck to open the door for Rebecca. After she climbed in, he closed the door and jogged around the front of the truck to get in the driver's side. They rode the short distance to the front of the park on a path wide enough for the truck Rebecca never noticed before. When they got there, he hopped out and opened the wooden gate and drove the truck through. He turned it off and looked to his right.

"I'm glad you came to talk to me."

"I'm glad you were here," she emphasized. For the second time in two days, she hugged someone she didn't know when she woke up because they had been through something traumatic together.

"I'm going to lock up the gate if you're all set."

They climbed out of their respective sides of the truck. Rebecca walked around the front and got into her car, putting the window down as quickly as possible, while Frank walked to the back to lock the gate.

"Keep asking those questions," Frank hollered over the sound of his truck engine.

"I will as long as you go see Chief Towne."

He finished with the gate and headed back to the truck. "I'm heading there now."

They drove away in the same direction and both turned right onto 3A. When they got into town, Frank turned into the police station and Rebecca continued driving to the library. While it may have been closed on a

Sunday, she couldn't stand the thought of all those books waiting in the drop box until tomorrow. Plus, working in the library would give her time to think about her next move. It was still her day off, and there were plenty of daylight hours remaining.

Chapter 5

The Winner

THE LIBRARY WAS A SAFE SPACE FOR MANY PEOPLE IN town, but especially for Rebecca. If she needed to center herself or clear her mind, she'd go to the library and pick a new project to work on. Today, she figured she'd work on a new display. New displays were difficult to start or finish when patrons were coming and going.

She couldn't stop thinking about Elise the whole time she was checking in the books from the drop box – marathon runners, roads, driving, being followed. 'Have you been down this road before?' was the name for the next display she was designing in her head. The first book that came to mind was *A Bend in the Road* by Nicholas Sparks then *Death on West End Road*, a cozy mystery. She went through the library's computer to find other titles including road and even ordered some new indie books from Amazon.

Throughout the process of creating the display, she kept thinking about finding Elise's killer. The police certainly had their job to do, but what didn't they have enough manpower for? With the drop box emptied and the display finished, she sat in a comfy chair by the front window and looked through the Sunday paper. The library got the local and not-so-local papers for the patrons to browse, but there was no one to fight with for it today.

The headline above the fold was 'Local Lipman Lives Large.' A picture of Jenny on top of the podium, flowers in hand and a first-place medal around her neck, was featured on most of the front page. Rebecca read the interview about how she had always dreamed of winning a marathon and knew this was her year. It was then she realized that this interview would have been conducted before anyone knew the fate of Elise. She wasn't sure how they kept it out of the paper, but the death of Elise wasn't mentioned on a single page.

She got out of the plush chair, a more difficult feat than it had been even five years ago, and walked to the check-out counter to retrieve her phone. She sent off a text to Kenny.

Rebecca: How did you keep Elise's death out of the Sunday paper?

She went back to reading the paper at the counter, waiting for a response, and the phone promptly rang.

"A phone call? I must be pretty important." She had a grin that spread across her whole face.

"You are, and I'm not foolish enough to answer that question in a text."

"Because I might take it to the paper, right?"

"No, because you never know who might get ahold of your phone or steal it on purpose now that we are officially a couple. I take your safety just a seriously as I take my daughters' safety." The huge grin transformed into a small pouty-lip smile with crinkly eyes. He was just a dream of a man.

"So, what's the answer?"

"We made a deal that they would hold out on publishing anything until Monday to give us a chance to do more detective work with the condition that we gave them an exclusive interview for the Monday paper."

"And have they interviewed you yet?"

"I'm on my way there now. I have the phone on speaker in the cruiser."

The headquarters for the paper was on the second floor of a brick office building known as the Rollins' Block. The building had been in the center of town since the end of the nineteenth century. The paper wasn't printed in town, but the reporters worked out of this space to always have a place to come together and be accessible to the public. They were one of the few newspapers that still printed a local publication.

Rebecca asked, "Are you still reviewing footage, or have you moved on?"

"Some officers are out looking for houses and businesses with video from the day while the rest of us are watching what we have and taking copious notes. Thanks for sending Frank, by the way. I only wish we had extra eyes to get through the footage faster when things like Frank show up."

"Too bad I can't help." She waited to see if he would take her up on the offer. "Want to have dinner tonight?" Rebecca asked. "Are the kids with Heather still?"

"They are, and I would love that. Want to eat out?"

"That would be lovely. Meet you somewhere or did you want to take one vehicle?"

"Let's meet at The Steadfast, if that's good for you. If I'm late, at least you can start without me."

Rebecca giggled. "Right. I might order an appetizer, but they've been going through bartenders at a pretty quick pace. I'm not ordering a mocktail." She knew Kenny would appreciate the joke based on how the summer had been going for the two of them.

"Understandable. I'll see you there for seven, okay?"

"It's a date! Bye." She ended the call, knowing he was driving.

Finding out he was headed to the newspaper office to be interviewed revealed that his time and attention was being pulled in different directions. Rebecca decided the only thing that made any sense at all was to talk to Jenny, something Kenny probably hadn't had time to do. When it came to motive, the person who benefits the most from a death is typically a suspect. While she wouldn't tell Jenny that's why she was there, the goal was to figure out if Jenny knew anything about Elise's death.

With summer over, many restaurants had already closed, but Jilly's wasn't one of them. With runners still in the area this morning, Rebecca was willing to bet they would be busy. She decided to wait a little longer and go near the end of lunch to pick up a take-out order. She continued to putter around the library, getting small tasks wrapped up here and there then called in an order for a chicken finger sandwich. It wasn't on the menu, but Rebecca had been eating it since she was a kid. The owner had changed since then, but she continued to make the simple sandwich with cranberry sauce on a hamburger bun.

Just before noon, she pulled up in front of Jilly's Restaurant. She stepped up and into the business that was a staple of the Newfound region. From families that came back year after year to bikers passing through, Jilly's was part of everyone's favorite food memories. When she got to the cash register, Jenny was there to ring her up.

"Good morning, Rebecca. How's your day going?" she said with a smile. She keyed in the price of the sandwich with fries and accepted the money Rebecca handed across the counter.

"Nowhere near as good as yours. Congratulations on your marathon win yesterday. You said it; it was your year." Jenny counted out the change and handed it to Rebecca.

"Thank you very much. I felt like nothing could stop me. It was the best run I've ever had."

"Want to sit down and chat for a minute? Do you have time?"

She looked around at the remaining customers and must have deduced that she had time, walking around the end of the counter and sitting at the last table with booths. "Why not?"

Rebecca joined her with the Styrofoam container. "Jenny, I was wondering what you heard about Elise."

Jenny's face fell, and the glow she once exuded disappeared as if a rain cloud now sat above her head. "Just rumors that her body was found yesterday. I've received at least a dozen messages asking me about her, but I don't know anything. I was running the race ahead of Elise. How would I know what happened?"

"You've got to know that people will wonder. Kennedy was out because of her surgery, and Elise was killed. Clearly, you had no control over Kennedy's injury, but for Elise to also go out... Do you know what people are saying?" Rebecca was making this up on the fly. She hadn't planned to go this route, but a made-up story to get a reaction might just have been worth it.

She sunk down low and whispered, "What are people saying?"

"That you might have had something to do with her death to help your chances of winning. I'm sorry I was the one to tell you."

Jenny slouched in the booth, one hand on her forehead and a shocked look on her face. "People think that of me?"

"It's just a rumor, and there wasn't even anything in the paper this morning. I'm not sure how people found out, but it had to have just been the gossip mill. There were a lot of people at the finish line, and it's hard to contain anything with cell phones now." Rebecca was getting the sense that Jenny really knew nothing about Elise's death. With her face turning a greenish color, it

43

seemed feasible she'd be running to the bathroom any minute.

"What could people possibly think I did? I passed her before Grey Rocks and only saw her one other time after I made the turn at Sculptured Rocks. I had the lead car with me, so someone would have seen me if I did anything."

"She wasn't found until after that part of the race, so I don't think anyone is accusing you of physically pushing her. Besides, I was the one who found Elise. It was pretty clear to me she was hit by a car."

Jenny looked up with a slack jaw and wide eyes. "Aww, Rebecca, I had no idea. How did you find her?"

"When you ran by me and Kennedy at the Shanty's water table, we were watching for Elise. When she didn't show up for five minutes or so, we got nervous and started trying to find out if anyone knew where she was. No one did, so the two of us walked the course backward looking for her." Jenny was listening intently. "She was found behind some rocks with damage to her head. It was a really bad scene."

Jenny nodded in silence until Rebecca stopped. "What made you think she was hit by a car?" Rebecca felt like this was confirmation that Jenny was innocent or at least didn't have knowledge of the details. She had told a lie, but Jenny reacted authentically to the lie and not the real scene. Had someone done this on purpose for Jenny, Rebecca figured they would have given her the details after. Rebecca knew this whole line of questioning might come back to bite her and damage her friendship with Jenny later, but she had to get to the heart of the matter.

"Based on where and how she was found, tripping or being pushed didn't make sense." She figured she'd leave it at that.

"What is Kenny, I mean Chief Towne, doing about it? You two are dating, right?"

"We don't talk about what he does for the police."

"Oh, right. Sorry."

"No offense taken. I think people make assumptions about us as well. I have thick enough skin and so does he." Rebecca had been slightly humorous in her response, but she straightened her face for the next part. "Is there anyone who might have done something to Elise on your behalf, even if you didn't ask them to or know about it? A big fan? A family member who wanted to see you win?"

"Do you think I couldn't win on my own?" Jenny sat straight and inhaled deeply.

"Not at all. I was cheering you on before and during the race, but I know that's a question that's going to come up. Can you think of anyone who might think they were doing you a favor by improving your odds, with Kennedy out, that is?"

"I can't think of anyone. My family and friends were all at the turnaround, then they planned to drive back through Hebron to get to 3A because it would be less congested. I'm sure they all stayed together, but asking them would be no problem if it cleared my name. You can tell Chief Towne that."

"I can tell him what I think and information I gather,

he just doesn't tell me anything back, so I will pass that along to him. Thank you for that." Rebecca looked at the analog clock on the wall. "I'm so sorry. I kept you longer than I meant to. You've got to close, and I'm stopping you." She slid to the end of the booth and stood. Jenny did the same.

"Thanks for coming and clearing that up. I hope if you hear any more rumors, you'll be comfortable telling them you spoke to me."

"I will. Thanks for talking. Congratulations again." Rebecca lifted her Styrofoam container as a way to say goodbye and turned around. "See you later Reese," she hollered to the chef and owner in the kitchen.

"Oh, hey, Rebecca. Thanks for stopping in," she called from the back.

"See you both around."

And with that, she left Jilly's with no more answers than she had entered with.

Chapter 6

The Runner-Up

Rebecca took her boxed-up chicken finger sandwich and fries to Kelley Park to sit and think. She parked on the street, next to the community center building. When she got out, she walked across the street and down the hill to sit under the pavilion that had hosted the pasta potluck dinner Friday night. She never could have imagined she'd be sitting here today with another murder to solve and very few clues.

She hadn't heard from Kenny again, but figured there was no news to report. He probably finished his interview and went back to the station to continue looking at footage.

While she sat at a picnic table thinking about the facts of the case, Kennedy walked up.

"Funny running into you here." She gave double finger guns and then holstered her hands at her imaginary belt. "Get it? Running into you."

For good measure, Rebecca decided to play along.

"That was a good one," she attempted to say without sarcasm.

"What are you doing here, eating, alone?"

"The library is closed today, and Kenny is investigating Elise's death. I have a day off with no plans, which is rare. I picked up a sandwich at Jilly's and decided to think here."

Kennedy sat across from Rebecca. "Has he made any progress?"

Rebecca needed to make a decision and quickly. "They are reviewing camera footage from homes and businesses along the course. He said it's taking a long time. He can't tell me if they found anything on the footage or what they are looking for specifically." While Rebecca wanted to come up with a convincing story or lie to get a reaction, it just didn't make sense to bother; Kennedy had been with her the whole day.

"Of course not." She swung her ponytail over her shoulder and leaned in. "It makes sense that would be their first plan of attack. Back where Elise was killed, though, there can't be many options for cameras."

"I feel like we were there forever, and I never thought at the time to check the area for houses that might have cameras. Many delete the recordings after three hours, so I hope the police got to them quickly."

"Three hours? That hardly seems useful. What if you're not home when something happens, and you don't know to check the camera?"

"Mine sends a message to my phone when movement is detected. I can see the clip right then. I've never done it, but I think I can choose to save it. That would be good to know, huh?" Rebecca laughed and continued eating her sandwich.

"Well, we can only hope someone saved something. If not, what businesses could possibly have cameras?"

"Shanty's, but that's no where near the scene of the crime."

Kennedy nodded. "Seems like someone chose that area well or got really lucky."

"Funny you should say that. When we were there, I was thinking about someone choosing to kill Elise during the marathon. What kind of planning would you do if you wanted to attempt this crime?"

Kennedy quickly shook her head side to side and shifted away from Rebecca. "I wouldn't ever plan something like this."

"I mean hypothetically, not actually you," Rebecca soothed.

"I was starting to wonder if you forgot where I was all day." Her body relaxed. "I guess scouting the route would be the first step. The starting line and 3A are just too busy. There would be no way to get away with it unseen."

"That's what I thought," Rebecca agreed.

"Once you turn off 3A, that road would be pretty secluded."

"Did you ever feel it was unsafe?" Rebecca asked between bites.

"I did feel like cars weren't always as far away as maybe they could have been, but when two cars pass each other and a runner is near that area, it can be tight. If a person did hit a runner, it would be easy enough to play it off as an accident."

"Maybe that was the plan. If it wasn't an accident, the driver could have just acted distraught and claimed they had to choose between hitting the oncoming car or the runner."

Kennedy dropped her face into her hands. "Can you imagine being that driver?"

"I just can't. I want this to be an accident, but the guilt that driver is living with must be unbearable." Rebecca took her last bite, hoping Kennedy would fill the silence. When she didn't, Rebecca asked, "Was the rest of the course safer?"

"Once you got back toward Sculptured Rocks there was less traffic. The turnaround and that area was busy with onlookers and volunteers, so anything happening there would be seen. After the turnaround and you're on West Shore Road, there is a long stretch of loneliness. Not many spectators and lots of nothing – except the occasional car. I do see why it would be the best place to try something."

"Here's another scenario, though. If Elise had been in the lead or neck and neck with Jenny, she never could have been picked off. The car in front of her would have been witness to everything."

"Right, but you could still claim an accident. Who hasn't swerved because they looked down to change the radio song or pick up their coffee?"

Rebecca nodded. "That's true. You'd still be in

trouble and even face charges like involuntary manslaughter, but not as bad as premeditated murder." She got up to throw away her container. The fries were cold now, and she wasn't really that hungry. Dinner at the Steadfast tonight would be nice, and she didn't want to spoil her appetite for that.

"Heading out?" Kennedy asked.

"Yeah. Not sure what I'll do with the rest of my day, but I'm going to drive around for a bit. You?"

"Oh, I was about to go for a run when I spotted you. I'll start my warm-ups again and then hit the pavement. Need to start training for next year."

"Never too early. However, it would be for me. I don't plan to run a marathon in this lifetime, or I'd be the victim."

"Of what?"

"Dropped dead from exhaustion or running out of breath." She giggled at her own joke and Kennedy joined her.

"Never too late. If you wanted someone to train with, I'd be happy to help."

The two women headed up the hill to where Rebecca had parked. Rebecca opened her car door and Kennedy started stretching on the sidewalk.

"Have fun," Rebecca said with a snarky undertone.

Kennedy changed up her stretching. "I will. Bye."

Rebecca sat down in the driver's seat, closed the door and started up her car. She pulled out of the space and waved to Kennedy as she drove off.

She made the decision to drive the course so she

could see what Kennedy was talking about. When she volunteered, she only saw the finish area and the water station she worked at. In previous years, she hadn't even seen that much, being stationed at the finish line to hand out bananas and waters.

She felt that Kennedy was right about 3A. The road was wide open, people and businesses were everywhere, and it would be hard to lie about something being an accident with all that space. She turned left to head through Danbury and toward Sculptured Rocks in Groton, a series of narrow, sharply carved rock formations on the Cockermouth River. When the water levels were normal, this was a popular area for swimming and relaxing in the cold water. This road would possibly allow for an 'accident,' but she wondered on race day how many bystanders would gather so they could see the marathon runners pass in both directions.

Next, she turned onto West Shore Road and traveled the long stretch on the western side of the lake. Knowing what she did about the part she volunteered at with Shanty's, so many cottages and vacation homes, this was the best side for someone to plan an attack on a runner. It also happened to be the stretch, she felt, where a real accident was most likely to happen. Without additional evidence or a confession, someone might get the proverbial slap on the wrist when they deserved to be in jail for life.

When she came upon the spot where she found Elise's body just yesterday, she passed it slowly, checking the area around it. Feeling like she needed to see it again, she pulled into a nearby driveway and turned around, taking another pass. She crept along, peering in all directions for possible cameras. Now that she was headed in the wrong direction, she pulled into a different driveway to turn back around to head home.

There were a few other areas that may have worked if someone was planning an attack, but she could see why they used the location they did. That made her think about something that just occurred. Though she wasn't scoping out a location to commit a crime, she did do something the actual killer may have done.

She drove until she reached Shanty's where she knew a text message would go through. She sent Kenny a text telling him to call her, then pulled back onto the road, hoping she would get reliable service before he actually returned the call.

Her phone vibrated about four minutes down the road. She answered and put it on speaker phone so she could continue driving – the road didn't have enough room to pull off without being on someone's property.

"Hey. What are you looking for when you watch the footage you have?" she asked quickly.

"Good afternoon. How are you?" he responded.

"Seriously, I'm fine, but I don't want to waste your time."

"What do you think we are looking for?" He had to balance what he was allowed to tell her as his girlfriend and what he couldn't tell her because she wasn't a police officer.

"I was driving by the location where I found Elise

and had to pull into two driveways to get a look at it. The first time I came up on it too quickly, so I didn't get a good look. Then I turned around. When I went by the second time, I got a better look going slower, but was now facing the wrong direction. I had to turn around in another driveway to go the direction I wanted to be going."

"What are you getting at?"

"Are you only looking for vehicles with damage, or are you looking for vehicles that are showing up multiple times?"

"We are looking for one of those things. Give me some more of your thought process."

"I talked to Kennedy about the course as a runner. It made me think about someone planning the murder. They'd need to scope out areas that would work, but what if you drove by and the runner wasn't there yet or had already passed one of your locations. The driver would need to turn around, possibly several times. They would need to do the same thing when they were planning."

"You're thinking we need to look for any repeat vehicles in the videos, and possibly look back before the day of the marathon," Kenny recapped.

"Exactly. So, I guess you *were* only looking for vehicles with front-end damage."

"That may have been a primary focus, but I'll pass along your theory and talk to the officers who have been watching the footage. They may have already seen the killer and not known it."

"Right. I saw Elise, and I'm not sure there would be a

lot of damage to a vehicle, especially if it was a higher riding vehicle like an SUV or a truck."

Kenny sighed loud enough on his end for her to hear it throughout her car. "So, my non-trained girlfriend may have just narrowed down a very significant difference in the way we investigate a crime with little to no evidence and thought to preserve evidence at the scene of the crime so emergency personnel didn't destroy it."

"Sounds about right to me." She drove her car down 3A, back in the direction of the finish of the marathon on the way to her house, her shoulders back and chin held high.

"I'm starting to think I should hire you."

"I'd never give up my job at the library. My hours are better, and I have less stress."

"Are we still on for dinner at the Steadfast for seven?" he checked.

"I'll meet you there. See ya later." She blew him a kiss over the phone.

"See you at seven."

Chapter 7

The Dinner

REBECCA FINISHED HER DRIVE HOME TO CHECK ON Joey and Bean. They were the best cats a woman could ever dream of. Her curtains and furniture still looked as good as the day she brought them home. They rarely threw up because they were indoor cats and, as far as she knew, didn't have access to mice in her house – at least not on the floors they were allowed access to. When she was down, they always knew just how to support her.

After walking through the door, the rubbing and purring commenced. She dropped to the floor to enjoy the love. If Rebecca stayed home all day, the cats would sleep around the house as if she wasn't there. The stack of sofa blankets, the window hammock and the hard floor were all better options than her lap. The exception to the rule of ignoring her during the day was coming home from work, or in this case, sleuthing. Evening snuggles were a completely different story.

After several minutes of belly and chin rubs, she

walked to the kitchen, dodging paws and tails along the way. She offered treats on the kitchen floor so she could easily put the wet food in dishes. Once the water was also changed, she made her way upstairs.

Picking out an outfit that didn't include cats or books was always a challenge. Kenny never said anything, but she figured it might do her well to add some neutral items to her wardrobe for dates at least.

Come to think of it, she didn't want to change who she was because she was in a relationship. Going to the wedding was one thing, but going on a date was her personal time, and she was going to dress in the way that she wanted. Kenny knew exactly who he was getting when they started dating because of all the time they spent together as friends after his divorce.

She went through the stack of shirts she typically wore to work or around the house. Her mental compromise was a subtle Harry Potter shirt with her house crest featuring a bronze eagle. Too many people got things wrong when it came to the houses, but she was a purist to the source material. Paired with fitted gray capris and wedge flip flops, she felt comfortable and stylish.

Now, what to do with the rest of her day off. The house was clean, and the library was all ready for tomorrow. She decided that a little research never hurt. Following news on runners wasn't something she did on a regular basis, so she went and got her laptop to check the internet for information on the trio that finished on the podium last year.

She used her computer at home so rarely, she actually

had to search for the power cord because the battery was dead. Once everything was sorted, she used a search engine to find articles from last year. This year's marathon had only been over for just over twenty-four hours, so she figured there wouldn't be as much information yet.

Last year, Elise Trussell was the top finisher, earning a personal best and qualifying for the Boston Marathon. She finished the Boston Marathon, but nowhere near the top. She was quoted as saying she would return the following year, 'stronger, faster and better than ever.' Unfortunately for her, that wouldn't be possible. Elise had been living with her parents. She had graduated from college but dedicated most of her time to training. Based on the information in the article, they were very supportive and in no rush to kick her out.

As Rebecca already knew, Kennedy Wright had placed second last year and couldn't run this year. The article was written long before the injury that caused the surgery, so she was talking about how she was the best runner she had ever been and was able to focus on training in a way she couldn't when she was in high school. She knew the odds were stacked against her, but she planned to, 'take out the competition with her mental strength.' That statement hadn't aged well. Kennedy was lucky she spent the day with Rebecca. She did mention that her boyfriend was her biggest supporter, but Rebecca didn't remember any mention of a boyfriend when they were volunteering. That would be something to look into or ask Kenny about. When Rebecca continued her search, she found a more recent article in The Record, the local paper, that she would miss out on the Boston Marathon and be granted a guaranteed spot the next year because of her knee. "I guess that's what she was training for when I saw her in the park," Rebecca said to herself.

The third-place finisher became the winner this year. Previously, Jenny Lipman had to fight tooth and nail to get her name mentioned for anything other than her age. Every article led with how she was beating the odds. It was as if a woman was almost on her death bed after forty. As a divorced mom of two, she should be working and taking care of her kids, according to the articles written by men, but was an inspiration to women who wanted it all, according to the articles written by women. Jenny had figured out how to work from home at night and train during the day while her kids were in school. When the kids were with their father on the weekends, she worked at Jilly's, but Rebecca knew that firsthand. She couldn't figure out how to get enough sleep as an unmarried woman with no children; Jenny really was an inspiration.

Her research on Jenny made Rebecca give a little more thought to how things might change as her relationship progressed with Kenny. He came with two young daughters. They would be part of their lives forever, but in the house for more than ten years still. Dating Kenny, as they were, consisted of one commitment, but helping to raise two daughters would require a completely different level. Not only did Kenny come with Melanie and Megan, but he also had an ex-wife and years of memories with her. Moving beyond where they were now would take some extra thought.

The last thing she found in her online research, if you could call it research, was that Jenny had beaten Elise in the Boston Marathon. Their overall times were vastly different, much more than their New Hampshire Marathon finish times. Even if Elise could beat her on their home turf, Boston was a horse of a different color. The New Hampshire marathon was described as 'rolling hills but a relatively easy end to the race' while the Boston Marathon had Heartbreak Hill near the end. That was the demise of Elise last year. This year, her demise was a little more final. It was clear there was a lot of history between these two runners that Kennedy hadn't been able to be a part of.

The research didn't take all afternoon, so she found a book she had been wanting to read for some time. She loved a good police procedural, the grislier the better, and was ready to crack the spine of *The Time Keeper* by Marissa Farrar. When the phone vibrated on the coffee table after a couple hours on the couch, her two reading companions both jumped and ran.

She tapped the button to accept the call. "Good evening," she purred. She had never purred before to anyone, so that tone was a shock to even her.

"Want to move dinner up to six? I need a break and will go back in after dinner."

"I can do that." She looked at the clock. The drive was less than ten minutes, but that meant dinner was in twenty. She could be out the door in under ten if she got off the phone. "I'll see you there. Bye."

"Rushing me off the phone so quickly?"

"A girl needs to get ready, and you left me no time."

"Just come as you are. I know what you look like in sweats. Get a table for us."

"See you soon." He ended the call first, and she realized she only needed to grab her bag and put on shoes. She did both of those things and grabbed the book she had been reading as well. She'd probably be able to sneak in one more chapter while she waited for him to arrive.

Sitting in the bar area with a non-alcoholic strawberry daiquiri felt pretty safe. The bartender had been there for a few years, so she felt even better about that. Her experience with bartenders, as of late, had been sketchy. She sipped at the drink and read in the corner.

Kenny appeared at the hostess stand, presumably asking if there were any solo diners who had already been seated. Rebecca watched to see what he did. In his police uniform, standing straight and tall, he turned to scan the bar area when the hostess shook her head. He located her quickly, and she stood to meet him halfway.

"Why didn't you get us a table?" He looked and sounded concerned with a furrowed brow.

"Because they have plenty of tables. We'll be seated immediately, and I already have my drink and know what I want. I won't take too much of your time tonight," she reassured.

"Thank you. Now that we're going back over all the footage based on your suggestion, it's all hands on deck."

He next spoke quietly and directly into her ear. "I may not have given you credit. I don't want anyone to know we've talked about the case."

"I completely understand. I never need credit. If I can be of help and the case moves along, that's the best-case scenario."

"Two for dinner, please," he told the hostess.

"Right this way." She walked the couple through the former home that had been built before eighteen hundred. They were seated next to floor to ceiling windows that looked out over the backyard. Twinkling lights gave the area an ethereal feel on the other side of the glass, almost as if it were part of a different world.

They both opened and closed the menu within a minute, as if they were merely checking that their chosen entrée was still there. When a waiter came over and asked about drinks, they were ready.

"What can I get for you this evening, Chief Towne?" Kenny looked up and into the face of the man wearing a white shirt and black pants. He looked young, maybe in his mid-twenties.

After examining him for a bit, he asked, "How do I know you, or rather, how do you know me?"

"I went to the high school down the road. You did several talks about drugs and safety when I was a kid."

"I'm sorry, I don't remember your name."

"It's Barrett. I was pretty quiet then."

"Did you sit in the back, near the windows?"

Barrett's face lit up. "I did." His reaction seemed much bigger than the situation. "My girlfriend was

Kennedy Wright in high school, and we've been off and on since then."

Slowly, Kenny turned to look at Rebecca. He double checked the menu then said, "I remember her as well. So nice to see you again. I don't mean to be rude..." He was cut off by Barrett.

"No problem at all. What can I get you."

Kenny ordered the Steak Oscar and Rebecca ordered the Lobster Mac & Cheese. She hoped to have leftovers for lunch tomorrow at the library.

"I'll put your order right in. Trying to get back to the station tonight?" he asked as he was turning to leave.

"Yes. Still a lot to do in the death of the marathon runner."

"Elise? I know. So awful. I'll get you out of here in a jiffy so you can get back to it." He trotted off and around a corner.

"Well, that's the boyfriend I was going to tell you about," Rebecca stated as if the wind had been taken from her sails.

"Why would you tell me about him?"

"Last year, she was interviewed and mentioned a boyfriend who was her biggest supporter, but when she was at the water station with me, he never came up. Someone picked her up, but I didn't think anything of it."

"Well, I'll take a look into him. Find anything else I should know about?"

She recapped the details of her online research, but the only thing worth noting was that Jenny had beaten

Elise in the Boston Marathon. Otherwise, most of it was information she already knew.

"Let's enjoy our evening now that we have business out of the way." He clinked his water glass with her fancy red frozen beverage, and they chatted about the girls and the library for about an hour before he had to get back to work. Both Kenny and Rebecca cleared their plates, so there were no leftovers to take home.

"Thank you for a night out. This was an unexpected treat," Rebecca said as he walked her to her car.

"Thank you for accepting my invitation." They shared a brief kiss before she slid into the driver's seat with the door held open.

"Unless I am mistaken, I asked you out to dinner," Rebecca clarified.

"I stand corrected, and I'll talk to you tomorrow. Let me know if your research turns up anything else."

"Will do, Chief!"

He closed the door and walked away. She drove home and promptly got ready for bed with her book.

Chapter 8

The Parents

Rebecca had intended to read until she fell asleep, but she ended up just staring at the ceiling for a long time. She wondered how to help with the investigation since she had no access to the video footage. While no one really knew what they were looking for, she thought she could be another set of eyes. She felt that maybe she had hinted at that to Kenny, but he didn't bite. He was as 'by the book' as one could be. It was surprising that he talked about the cases at all with her.

Mentally, she went through a list of people immediately adjacent to Elise. Obviously, Kennedy and Jenny were her most recent competitors, but both had alibis. Next, she recently learned that Kennedy had an on-again-off-again boyfriend. Kenny was looking into him, so she wasn't going to be of any help there. Elise had been a transplant, not landing in the Newfound area until after college, so there weren't any locals that had a long-standing feud over something that happened in high school.

Rebecca gave a single snort in place of a full laugh. She realized it was refreshing that this wasn't about high school drama. Having gone through the Newfound School District herself, she was relieved to not be interviewing people she had known since elementary school this time.

When it came to Jenny, it was obvious that the kids would have been with their father. Rebecca could just about guarantee there would be pictures of them at the medal ceremony in addition to other candids. Since the race was on a Saturday and they were too young to be alone, this was a logical conclusion to make.

There were only two people remaining who had a connection to this mystery but hadn't been assessed by Rebecca, and they were Elise's parents. They weren't old as far as she was concerned, but they weren't young either. Shirley and Ralph Trussell owned the town's flower shop, *What in Carnation*, in the same parking lot as the fitness center Rebecca tried yoga at for the first time. Rebecca was very familiar with them as she would often pick up flowers for the check-out counter. They moved to the Newfound area shortly after Elise got her new ranger job.

Ralph had owned a very successful flower business in Boston, he told Rebecca on one visit. He was done with the fast pace of life in the neighboring state and wanted to slow down without retiring. Elise getting the job at Wellington was just the motivation he needed to sell what he had and downsize. Shirley was just along for the ride. She had been the primary parent for her daughter growing up and started helping at Ralph's shop when Elise went off to college. It kept her busy enough to not get bored, but she told Rebecca once that she really missed the city life.

The library could always use a new bouquet, and it would allow her to visit Ralph and Shirley, if they were even open. Owning a business, especially in the service industry like they were, meant it was hard to close. They didn't have any other employees to keep the place running if they were taking time to grieve, so she felt it was quite probable they would be working.

When she woke on Monday morning, she checked her phone for the time. "Nine!" she shouted and proceeded to jump from the bed, along with Joey and Bean. She ran to the bathroom to throw her hair up in a messy bun and brush her teeth. Returning to the bedroom, she quickly dressed in a pair of capris and whichever book shirt was on the top of the clean laundry in the hamper. She hadn't been to the library since Friday, so even if she repeated a shirt, it was last worn at least a few days ago.

Joey and Bean followed her down the stairs as she surprised even them by sprinting through her bedroom doorway. They still made it to their food bowls in time to watch her scoop out the fancy tuna cat food into their dishes. She added some dry food to the neglected bowls and changed their water. "Sorry, guys. I've got to go."

The Subaru sat in the driveway, ready to take her on

her next big adventure. As she drove to the florist, fingers crossed that they were open, it registered that all of the thinking she did last night must have kept her up later than she realized. Sleeping in until nine was not a common occurrence.

Rebecca pulled up to the one traffic light in town and waited her turn to pull into the parking lot for *What in Carnation* and the fitness center. The small neon sign was illuminated in the front window of the florist shop, and one car sat parked four spaces from the front door. She parked in the fifth spot, not wanting to take up one of the best spaces in case of a sudden rush for flowers.

A light tinkling sound caused Shirley to pop up from behind the counter. "Good morning. Welcome to *What in Carnation.* How can I help you today? Oh, hi, Rebecca."

Rebecca recognized the fake smile and bloodshot eyes immediately. "Shirley. How are you?"

"Don't ask me that or I'll cry, and I don't think I have any tears left." She took long deep breaths to regain the control she had painted on before Rebecca had entered the shop. "We're holding things together for the shop, but as soon as we are alone, the grief is overwhelming."

"I'm sure it is." Rebecca had no way of knowing just how terrible it would be to lose your only child still in their twenties, but she'd say anything right about now to support Shirley. "Where is Ralph?"

"In the back. I told him I'd take care of the customers if he took care of the flowers."

"Any chance you two can take a few days off?"

"There's no point. If we're here, at least we have something else to think about. We had already ordered product before the weekend that came in this morning, so it would just rot if we weren't open."

Rebecca figured she'd order her flowers now to give Ralph something to do. "Well, I would love to take some of those flowers off your hands for the library, if I may." She tried to balance the happy tone in her voice with a sense of compassion for what they were going through.

"We'd love to put something together. Is it for the front desk?" Shirley smiled a small but real smile. Clearly, this did take her mind off the horrible events, even if just for a split second.

"I'd like one vase for the front desk and one to go in the front window, please."

"Did you have a type of flower or color in mind?"

"Why don't you ask Ralph what he thinks will last the longest so the library can get the best bang for their buck."

Shirley nodded and went through a curtain to the back of the shop. She was only gone for about a minute when she returned with Ralph at her side. He held up two stems. "Rebecca," he said, giving her a single bob of the head. "Would you like to go with dahlias, sunflowers or a variety of native flowers in fall colors?"

"Since they won't be near each other, can I get one vase with a variety of dahlias and the other whatever native varieties you have in fall colors?"

"I can do that. Be right back." Without an ounce of

visible emotion, he retreated to the safety of the room behind the curtain.

Shirley looked at Rebecca. She whispered, "I'm sorry for his demeanor. He's still in shock."

"I don't think anyone would expect anything different."

"He blames himself."

Rebecca didn't know how to even begin to process those three words. "Why? How?"

"In the past, he's watched her run and moved along the course to cheer her on. This year, she wanted us to be at the finish line, surprised if she won instead of knowing exactly how it was going all along the way. We agreed because that's what she wanted. She said sometimes it was distracting to see us during the race. We stood at the finish line and watched Jenny win then waited. We waited so long before the police came and got us."

"You and Ralph can't possibly hold yourselves accountable for this. Being on the course couldn't have stopped it from happening." Rebecca spoke the truth, though she didn't know if it was helping.

"But Elise had mentioned a couple times she felt like she was being followed home, and we just blew it off. It didn't make any sense. She's not famous. She doesn't have any crazy ex-boyfriends. Now, we're wondering if we should have taken her feelings seriously."

"Did she say anything about who was following her or a type of vehicle?"

Distraught, Shirley just kept talking. "She said a truck or SUV, something big. They followed her from the gate at Wellington, she thought, almost to the house. There's no reason to go all the way out to where we live from Wellington and then just stop and turn around. Why didn't we have her report it to the police?" Shirley broke down.

Ralph came running out. "What's wrong? What happened?"

"Shirley was telling me that Elise thought someone was following her. Did she give you any details?"

"She said it didn't have a front plate, and I found that odd." Ralph held Shirley as she cried quietly. "One of the times it got up close when she had to stop at an intersection. I told her it was probably just a lost tourist. I'll never forgive myself for not going to the police that night."

"Do you know how long ago that was?" Rebecca put the brakes on how eager she was to get more information if there was any. "I mean, was it recent?"

"It was only a couple nights before the marathon."

"Do you remember what intersection?"

Shirley picked her head up off Ralph's chest. "Why are you asking so many questions?"

"Well, you said you wished you had gone to the police, right? Does that mean you haven't told them any of this?"

The couple looked at each other. "They didn't ask for specifics."

"*Do* you have specifics?" Rebecca asked, with emphasis on the first word.

"She said it was at the intersection of West Shore Road and 3A. Why does it matter?"

"Any chance you can deliver those flowers to the library when you have time today? I'll leave my card with you, but I want to call Chief Towne with your information. I'm sure he'll stop by as soon as he can, but this could be really important."

"Yes, I'll bring them myself," Ralph stated. "If you can help in any way, we'd appreciate it."

"Just charge my card for the flowers and drop it off when you deliver them, okay?" She didn't wait for an answer. Not only had she realized how close it was to opening time for the library, but she also wanted to call Kenny to let him know what she had learned.

It was a good thing the drive from the flower shop to the library was brief because she didn't want to forget a thing. As soon as the doors were unlocked and the books from the drop box were dumped on the counter, she dialed Kenny's number.

"Good morning, beautiful," he said after answering quickly. "Did you sleep well?"

"No, and it's a good thing. I just left *What in Carnation*, and I spoke with Shirley and Ralph."

"Rebecca." He dragged out her name. No doubt, there was a little bit of an eye roll with it. "They are grieving parents. We already spoke with them, anyway."

"Someone talked to them and didn't get everything. Do you want to know what I know, or do you want to make finding this person harder for yourself."

"You know the answer to that." Kenny waited silently on the other end of the call. "Rebecca, what do you know?"

"Please?"

"Please get on with it," he huffed.

"Ralph told me a couple nights before the marathon, he didn't nail it down more than that, Elise was followed."

"He told us that too."

"What he didn't tell you, I believe, was that the truck or SUV didn't have a front plate."

"How does he know that?" She could hear the squeaky chair in the background, as if he sat up or moved suddenly in his chair at the police station.

"He said she told him when the truck got up close at the intersection of West Shore Road and 3A, she could see it didn't have a front plate. Any chance the place on the opposite side of that intersection has a camera?"

"I know we have footage from them on the day of the marathon, but I'll go right now to see if they have any previous footage still. You're amazing!"

"Don't forget to tell who ever is looking at day-of footage as well. We don't know the color, but a truck or SUV with no front plate should narrow down what we're looking for. I mean, what you're looking for." She realized she was telling the professional how to do his job, but she could apologize for that later.

"I'm on it. Keep in touch if you and Mary solve the case for us this morning."

"Will do, Chief."

Chapter 9

The Memory

REBECCA HUSTLED AROUND THE LIBRARY. THERE were no special events, but she wanted to get onto the computer every chance she could. There might be more articles or photographs to help her assist the police officers in solving this mystery. With them all watching video footage of the mystery vehicle, she might be the only set of eyes searching the internet for clues. Having now decided there was no way this was an accident, she was fully focused on getting this wrapped up quickly.

Mary arrived at noon, on time, as she always did on Mondays. While she was a volunteer and not required to be there at a specified time, she liked having the structure. When she entered, she was carrying the newspaper and the two cozy mysteries she checked out on Friday.

"Rebecca, dear, you left the paper outside this morning. You're lucky no one took it."

"It was quite the morning. I overslept and stopped at

the florist. Ralph is coming by later with my bouquets. I was running so late I just left my credit card with him and asked him to return it when he dropped off my order."

Mary checked in the two cozies and placed the newspaper on the counter, opening it at the fold so she could see the front but hadn't looked down at it yet. "But why did you spend money on flowers? I would have gladly brought fresh ones from my garden for free." She looked down at the front page and gasped. "Rebecca, have you seen this? Of course, you haven't. I just brought it in. Come look."

Knowing exactly what she was going to see, Rebecca took three steps and looked over Mary's shoulder. 'Hit and Run at the Marathon' was the headline. Sunday's paper had been all about the runners who took home medals, but the Monday paper was all about the death of Elise Trussell.

"How tacky," Mary stated. "That headline should never have made it past the editor."

"Headlines sell papers. I'm not surprised." Mary continued to read the paper, so Rebecca returned to the computer.

After a couple minutes passed in silence, Mary asked, "Rebecca, did you know Chief Towne was interviewed for this article?"

"Yes. I'm actually surprised they didn't seek me out. Maybe they will today. It's not like I can hide."

"Why would you hide, dear, and why would they seek you out?"

Apparently, Rebecca hadn't been named in the article.

Mary continued, "Says here, Kennedy Wright, the woman who came in second last year, found the body of Elise Trussell along the course. She was interviewed."

"I was the one with Kennedy when we found the body. I actually discovered Elise first and Kennedy just couldn't handle it. Do you mind if I read the article? I'd love to know Kennedy's version."

Mary handed over the paper. "How are you doing? That couldn't have been easy for you."

"I'm doing as well as can be expected. That's actually why I went to buy flowers this morning. Ralph and Shirley are the parents of Elise. I wanted to see if they knew anything that could help." She placed the newspaper on the counter next to the computer.

"Did they?"

"Actually, there were some details I already shared with Kenny that could narrow down what they are looking for in the video footage they collected, but there's just so much of it. With new information, I fear they'll have to look at some of it all over again."

"Well, if you're trying to help them, let me help you. Is there anything I can take off your plate?"

Rebecca thought for a moment. "Karen will be in tomorrow. Would you mind setting up the multi-purpose room for her, and I'll stay at the counter? I came in and did a bunch of work yesterday, so I think that's the only thing left at the moment." The thought crossed her mind that maybe she shouldn't ask Mary to do something like that, but she'd never once seen a physical task around the library Mary was too old to do. Even if she was in her eighties, which Rebecca had never confirmed, she planned to treat her just like any other volunteer unless Mary told her otherwise. Too often, society tried to place restrictions on people based on age that were built on false assumptions, and Rebecca was not going to be part of that.

"I'm on it." Mary took off her light cardigan and carefully placed it on the back of a chair behind the counter. "How many littles are we expecting?"

"Let's assume fifteen. If it's any different, I'll help Karen tomorrow while she's setting up the art activity."

"Has she told you what it will be this week?"

Rebecca laughed. "I think she's totally crazy, but she's planning to do fall leaf paintings where you paint the leaf and use it like a stamp. I hope parents bring their kids in with an apron or maybe a tarp."

"I think Karen knows what she's doing. I'll be out back if you need me." Mary turned and walked past the children's section and into the multi-purpose room.

Rebecca turned to the article in the paper. When she read Kennedy's account of the discovery, she was in shock. She was happy her name wasn't mentioned, but it was as if Kennedy told the story from Rebecca's point of view. She took credit for the idea of searching for Elise and stated she was the one to see the shoes first. Rebecca was beside herself.

The front door to the library opened, causing Rebecca to quickly dispose of the paper on the floor behind the counter. Ralph was carrying one of her vases full of the most beautiful fall colors. A variety of native flowers overflowed the glass container. He walked up to the check-out counter and set it down.

"Here is your card," he said as he handed over the plastic rectangle. "We appreciate your business. I'll go get the second one out of the car." He turned and walked away before Rebecca could respond. Based on this morning, he may be trying to avoid conversation, which Rebecca could respect. When he returned, the second vase was brimming with dahlias.

"Ralph, they are beautiful. Just what we needed to start celebrating fall without going straight to Halloween. Ralph had walked the vase over to the front window to set it down on a low table. He froze. Not only did he not respond to Rebecca, but he also didn't move. "Ralph, are you okay?" She walked around the counter and over near Ralph, not wanting to spook him. He was staring out the front window with both palms flat on the low table bracketed by two comfy chairs.

She waited for him to speak, and when he finally did, he said, "Chief Towne came to speak to us again, and I've just realized I forgot something Elise said about the vehicle following her."

"What was it?" Rebecca waited with bated breath, afraid she'd cause him to forget whatever epiphany he just experienced at the window.

"She said at first she thought it was a police vehicle because of the lights on top. She could see the reflection of her brake lights in them when she pulled up to the intersection, then noticed it didn't say anything on the hood and had no front plate. The front plate stuck in my memory, and I forgot about the light bar."

"What just made you think about it now?"

"I just saw a truck go by with a light bar, but I didn't notice if it had a front plate or not. Should I call Chief Towne?"

Rebecca already had her hand on the phone in her back pocket. She chose Kenny's number from the list of recent calls and waited for him to pick up, but he didn't. She knew he was at the station today, or at least he was earlier. She tried to call again. When he didn't answer a second time, she sent a text asking where he was. A response came quickly.

Kenny: I'm in a meeting. What's up?

Rebecca: New information from Ralph.

Rebecca: Please call ASAP.

Kenny: One minute

"Ralph, I'll have Kenny on the phone for you in one minute. Will you stay to tell him what you just told me?"

"Of course."

Other patrons entered the library and walked up to the counter, waiting patiently for someone to assist them. Holding the phone as if it was about to explode, she walked briskly to the multi-purpose room, letting the patrons know she'd be right back.

"Mary, can you come help at the desk? I have Ralph here with information for Chief Towne, and he's about to call me back. We may have our big break."

Mary wasted no time dropping the two stacked chairs

she was carrying from the closet to the tables in the center of the room. Moving at a speed Rebecca had yet to observe, Mary made her way to the counter in her beige orthopedic shoes.

"How can I help you ladies today?"

"Ralph," Rebecca said, gaining his attention. "Let's go back here." She gestured in the direction the multi-purpose room she had just come from. Together, they walked back and closed the door for privacy. Moments later, her phone vibrated in her hand, almost causing her to drop it.

She pressed the button to accept the call. "Kenny?"

"I'm here. Do you have Ralph with you?"

"I do."

"Hello, Chief Towne. Sorry to be such a bother."

"No bother at all. Anything that can help us bring your daughter's killer to justice is well worth my time. Now, Rebecca said you had some new information. What was it?"

Ralph recounted the story he had just finished telling Rebecca about the assumption the vehicle was police because of the light bar. "I only remember the rest of her account because I saw a white truck out the front window of the library as I was setting down the display of dahlias, and it had a light bar on top."

"You didn't happen to notice if it had a front plate or any damage, did you?"

"No, sir. I'm sorry."

"Nothing to be sorry about. I think I have everything I need. Will you be at the shop the rest of the day?"

He nodded then shook his head a bit, probably realizing Chief Towne couldn't see him. "I will. If you need me, just stop by."

"Perfect, and thank you for getting this new information to me as quickly as possible."

Rebecca put the phone at her side but didn't push the button to cancel the call. She walked Ralph back to the front doors and gave him a sympathetic hug after thanking him again for the beautiful flowers.

When he left and she picked the phone back up to her ear, she heard Kenny say, "Rebecca, you still there?"

"I'm here. What can I do?"

"Does the library still have the security camera above the front entrance that points out toward the road?" Kenny almost sounded out of breath, as if he was suddenly moving while still on the phone.

"We do."

"Pull up the footage from the last ten or so minutes. I'll be there in two." He disconnected the call, presumably so he could drive.

"Rebecca, Captain America is here," Mary announced around the women still standing at the counter.

Slightly surprised that Mary knew who Captain America was, Rebecca popped her head out of the office.

"In here."

Kenny walked into the office and closed the door behind him. "Please tell me you have the truck Ralph saw on the camera. Please tell me it is missing the front plate, but you got the back plate on the video. Please."

The pair stayed in the office together for several minutes. When he left, Chief town waved to Mary quickly as he jogged back to the cruiser parked just outside the entrance.

"Well?" Mary asked.

"I'm not sure yet, but he seemed to be pretty confident he's got what he needs. Fingers crossed."

Mary added, "Toes too."

Chapter 10

The Finish

THE COMMUNITY CENTER WAS HOSTING A celebration dinner at The Steadfast to recognize Jenny's win at the New Hampshire Marathon. They posted the details late Saturday night, allowing racers to buy tickets to the event first and then the general public. There wouldn't be many extras, so Rebecca was surprised when she received an invitation receipt via text message from Kenny later that afternoon. The dinner started at seven, and he stated that he would meet her there.

She was excited to celebrate Jenny's accomplishment along with her fellow runners, family and friends. Most runners left the next day, so this would be about the people who lived around Newfound Lake. The community always came together in times of need, but a huge achievement like this was a reason to celebrate.

At seven, Rebecca pulled into the parking lot after a quick shower and change, her wet hair wrapped up on top of her head and a slash of mascara the only attempts to look polished. She scanned the worn pavement for Kenny's cruiser and found it was the third car in from the driveway, facing the road. When she walked up the steps to the front door, a waiter was there to open it.

"Thank you," she said as she entered.

"My pleasure," the young man responded.

She noted that this young man was not the same one who had waited on them last night. She saw that young man, Barrett, as soon as she entered the space for the celebration. Kennedy Wright was on Barrett's arm near the curved windows that looked out over the parking area and the mountains in the distance. Her long ponytail swished from shoulder to shoulder as she carried on a lively conversation with another two couples.

Rebecca entered the space and looked for Kenny but didn't see him.

"Rebecca," Kennedy called out and waved vigorously. "Over here."

The other five faces in the group now looked in her direction while others in the space were looking at Kennedy.

Rebecca walked over to Kennedy, and they gave each other a brief hug.

"Rebecca, this is Barrett, my boyfriend." She then gestured to and introduced the couples she had just been chatting with.

"Is this the boyfriend who picked you up on Saturday in the Tacoma?" Rebecca decided to get right to the point.

"He did pick me up. How did you remember the truck?"

"Just a good memory, I suppose." Rebecca noted that Kennedy didn't seem affected by the topic of Saturday's pick-up, even though she was quite distraught at the time. "Nice truck, Barrett. Pretty new?"

Barrett dropped Kennedy's arm, looking fully focused on Rebecca. "Less than a year. My dad bought it and had a stroke, so he couldn't get in and out of it anymore. Let me take over the payments."

"Is your father local? Do I know him?"

"You might, but he lives in Florida now. He's also Barrett."

"I don't ever remember meeting a Barrett, but that's not to say I haven't. When you waited on us last night, I even mentioned to Chief Towne that I'd never met anyone with that name before." It sounded good, though she couldn't remember actually saying it out loud.

"Speak of the devil," Kennedy announced, louder than necessary.

Chief Towne had entered the dining room and was walking in their direction. He really did look good in that uniform, she thought.

"Good evening," he said to the group. Surprising Rebecca, he kissed her on the cheek. It still felt strange for him to show affection like that in public. There was nothing wrong with it, but there was a part of her that felt it wasn't appropriate for some reason.

"Attention, please. Can I have your attention please?" The owner of the Steadfast, Mr. MacDunn, attempted to get everyone to stop talking and pay attention to him. "I'd like to introduce you to the director of the community center, Morey Bornne." Everyone clapped as the woman with pale skin, freckles and ginger hair motioned for them to quiet down.

"We have been blessed to have so much local success this year and last year at the New Hampshire Marathon. While we deeply mourn the loss of Elise Trussell, we cannot let that dampen our celebration for this year's first-place finisher, Jenny Lipman." Her voice rose on the last name, trying to be heard over the hoots and hollers from the group of supporters.

Jenny entered the room with one child in her arms and the other in the arms of the man following her. Rebecca presumed this man was her ex-husband. Attending a function at seven with two small children would be difficult alone, so it only made sense that she had help. Behind them was an older woman carrying a large plastic tote of kids books and toys. If she were going to make a guess, she'd say this woman was probably a grandparent.

With the two children seated at a table with the man and older woman, Jenny stood next to Morey. "We are proud to have you represent us at the Boston Marathon this coming April, along with Kennedy Wright. Kennedy, why don't you join us?"

Kennedy bounded across the space and gave Jenny the same brief hug Rebecca had received. She then turned to beam at the faces scattered throughout the room, clearly proud of being included.

"This past year, Newfound was represented by Elise and Jenny, and this coming year, Jenny and Kennedy will represent Newfound at the Boston Marathon. We are blessed to have two wonderful representatives of our community. Knock 'em dead, ladies." As soon as the words left her lips, her face went a whiter shade of pale. Not coming up with replacement words fast enough, the crowd clapped to cover the error in judgement. When it was quiet again, Morey finished with, "Everyone, enjoy the evening."

Kennedy returned to the group of seven waiting to receive her, and Jenny joined her family at their table. Servers started coming around with passed appetizers, and Morey tried to scamper from the room.

Kenny leaned down to Rebecca's ear. "Go sit in the tavern." Without question, she excused herself from the group. She noticed Kenny started to head to the far wall of the room but didn't see what happened next. Moments later, he was joined by Jenny's ex-husband.

Kenny chose two tall wooden chairs at the bar, one empty seat away from where Rebecca sat.

"Joe. Do you mind if I call you Joe?"

The man seated on the far side of Kenny wrung his hands in his lap. "Joe is fine. What can I do for you, Chief Towne?"

"What you can do is tell me where you were on Saturday while Jenny was running the marathon."

"I had the kids in Kelley Park. We watched her start the race then killed time on the playground equipment. I mean, we were still there when she crossed the finish line. The first thing she did was hug the kids, her mother and then me."

"I know you're divorced, Joe, and that you moved to Arizona for a while. Are you two getting back together?"

"I hope so. Why?"

Kenny took an extended deep breath. "I want you to think long and hard about how you answer the next question, if you choose to answer it. You are not required to answer it. Do you understand?"

Joe nodded. "Yes," he responded and dropped his face to his hands still moving in his lap.

"Did you leave Kelley Park and drive on West Shore Road Saturday during the marathon?"

Joe didn't move or answer. He sat in the chair at the bar and stared at his hands.

"I am planning to arrest you tonight, and the officers in this room are going to assist me if you resist, but I'd like to give you a chance to tell your story. I brought you out here discretely so your kids don't see this, but you need to know that you will not be going home tonight."

Joe sat up as straight as possible while blowing out a thoughtful breath. He turned and looked straight at Kenny. Rebecca kept scanning from side to side to see as much of the interaction as possible without being disruptive.

"I took care of things so my wife would have better odds of winning and hopefully be happy enough to take me back, but I didn't work on this alone. I'm not going down without the person who thought up this stupid plan."

Kenny stammered, "What plan, and who are you accusing of creating it with you?" This was the first time Rebecca hadn't heard a confident and collected version of Chief Towne.

"Barrett."

"I'm sorry. You want me to believe Barrett helped you murder Elise so your ex-wife could have a better chance of winning the marathon. That doesn't make sense."

"Look, Kennedy and Jenny would both benefit from Elise being out of the race. It was never our goal to kill her. We both drove back and forth on West Shore Road, trying to find a time and location where we could give her a little nudge."

Kenny signaled to an officer who was quietly standing in a corner. That officer motioned to another to leave the tavern with him.

"I'm placing you under arrest. Are you going to go quietly so that your kids don't see you being forcefully removed?"

"I will." He hopped down from the chair and turned around with his hands behind his back. Kenny handcuffed him and walked out quietly. Rebecca got up to return to the dining room where she heard a lot of loud screaming.

Barrett, on the other hand, was in the process of making quite the scene. The two officers who left the tavern together were joined by a third and had Barrett face-down on the floor. Once handcuffed, they helped him up and escorted him out of the restaurant.

At this point, everyone was quietly trying to assess

the situation. Kennedy was in tears being attended to by two women. Jenny looked to be in shock, staring straight ahead while the grandmotherly figure distracted the children.

The dinner was served, but the celebration atmosphere was gone. People ate their food and attempted to pretend nothing was wrong. Kennedy left her entire plate uneaten, and Jenny was putting on a façade that convinced her small children, and no one else, that everything was fine. The entire group departed without dessert ever being served.

Tuesday morning, Rebecca woke when she wanted to. The extended hours of summer were behind her, and she had the morning off. She was disappointed that Catch of the Day was closed for the season. A quiet lunch on the lake with a good book sounded perfect for today. Alas, she wouldn't even have leftovers to settle for, having eaten all of it two nights ago.

She stayed in bed longer than usual, reading a book that had been recommended on a social media group. When she did get up, she only moved to the couch to flip through the channels but did not actually watch anything. When a mystery was finally solved, Rebecca had a hard time filling in the empty space in her day.

Eventually, she got dressed, noting that Karen would be in shortly. Having Mary set up the room yesterday was genius. If Karen needed help with supplies,

Rebecca could help with that instead of helping move furniture.

Once Rebecca was behind the counter and Karen was in the multi-purpose room, Kenny entered the library.

Rebecca scanned the space, even though she knew everyone else was behind a closed door in the back, and whispered, "Well?"

"Double confession. The two men agreed they were both willing to take the same risks in order to help the women they loved. Joe, however, broke the deal to take the fall without bringing the other down. That was the reason for Barrett's big explosion at the celebration. Their stories all check out. Both men were interviewed in separate rooms and told mostly identical stories. It was pure luck that both trucks were so similar. Had they not been, it would have been even harder to find the evidence we needed."

"Why would it be harder?"

"Based on information you collected, we were able to get evidence on both trucks all over West Shore Road without realizing it wasn't just one truck without closer inspection. If Joe hadn't given us Barrett, we probably would have assumed all of the footage was Joe because the size, description and color of the trucks were so similar."

"So, how did Joe end up being the actual killer?"

"Luck of the draw. He happened to be the one who was in the right place at the right time, so to speak. Elise didn't have any other runners nearby, and she was in one of the predetermined spots that was unlikely to have witnesses."

"Any other evidence?"

"The tire marks in dust you suggested we catalog on the road matched perfectly to Joe's truck. Good job, Ms. Ramsey."

"Good job to you too, Chief Towne."

"Now we just have one mystery left to solve."

"What's that?" Rebecca cocked her head to one side, thoroughly confused by this new development.

"How are we going to get the girls to decide on Halloween costumes that they still want to wear when it comes time to trick-or-treat?"

"We?"

"Yes. Heather and I talked about you helping on this one, really introducing you to the girls as part of the family. Are you in?"

Rebecca paused. "I'm in love. After all, ghouls just wanna have fun!"

PLEASE LEAVE A REVIEW!

★ ★ ★ ★ ★

Virginia K Bennett

An Appetite for Solving Crime

THANK YOU FOR READING MY BOOK!

I WOULD LOVE TO READ YOUR FEEDBACK ON
FACEBOOK, INSTAGRAM, AMAZON, OR
SIMPLY SEND AN EMAIL TO:

authorvirginiakbennett@gmail.com

Recipe

Crockpot Pasta Sauce
Ingredients:
28 oz. can of Crushed Fired Roasted Tomatoes
6 oz. can of Tomato Paste
1 TBSP Dried Basil
1 TBSP Dried Italian Seasoning
1 TBSP Dried Oregano
1 TBSP Garlic or Onion Powder
Salt and Pepper to Taste

Starting with tomatoes, empty all ingredients
into a 1.5 QT crockpot.
Use an immersion blender to remove all chunks, if
desired.
Turn on low for approximately 5 hours.
If adding fresh or frozen meatballs (from Book 1), cook
5½ to 6 hours.

Recipe

Serves sauce for 3 to 4 people.
Recipe is easy to double or triple with a larger crockpot.

About the Author

When she's not writing on her couch with her two cats, Twyla and Geo, Virginia is busy teaching middle school math, grocery shopping, cooking or spending time with her husband and son. Together, her small family loves to go geocaching and visit theme parks.

Mysteries have always been an interesting challenge for Virginia, much like watching a magician perform. Unless you want to hear the entire thought process behind who she thinks is the killer and why, you might want to avoid watching any movies together.

The path to publishing a book is different for everyone and her path is full of twists and turns. Thank you to those who support the journey.

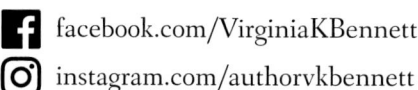

facebook.com/VirginiaKBennett

instagram.com/authorvkbennett

Made in United States
North Haven, CT
12 December 2023

45665604R00059